THIS WHERE'S WALDO? BOOK BELONGS TO:

HEY, WALDO FANS! FIVE INTREPID TRAVELERS ARE LOST IN EVERY SCENE! CAN YOU FIND THEM?

ODLAW   WIZARD WHITEBEARD   WENDA   WOOF   WALDO

AND IN EVERY SCENE, THE TRAVELERS HAVE EACH LOST SOMETHING PRECIOUS! CAN YOU FIND THESE ITEMS TOO?

WALDO'S KEY   WOOF'S BONE   WENDA'S CAMERA
WIZARD WHITEBEARD'S SCROLL   ODLAW'S BINOCULARS

For Elizabeth

First U.S. paperback edition 2011

Library of Congress Cataloging-in-Publication Data is available.
Library of Congress Catalog Card Number 2009012055

ISBN 978-0-7636-4725-4

10 11 12 13 14 15 SWT 10 9 8 7 6 5 4 3 2 1

Printed in Dongguan, Guangdong, China

This book was typeset in Optima and Wallyfont.
The illustrations were done in watercolor and water-based ink.

Candlewick Press
99 Dover Street
Somerville, Massachusetts 02144

visit us at www.candlewick.com

WHERE'S WALDO?

THE INCREDIBLE PAPER CHASE

MARTIN HANDFORD

CANDLEWICK PRESS

THE JURASSIC GAMES
GOODNESS CRETACEOUS! WHO WILL YOU SUPPORT FROM THE SIDELINES: THE BLUE STRIPY-SAURUS TEAM OR THE PINK SPOTTY-DOCUS TEAM? WILL YOU CHEER FOR CRICKET, ROWING, OR BASKETBALL? DON'T FORGET TO WAVE IF YOU SEE A T. REX – THEY'RE NOT ON ANY TEAM, BUT YOU WOULDN'T WANT TO GET ON THEIR BAD SIDE!

PICTURE THIS

PHEW! LOOK AT ALL THESE FRAMED PORTRAITS. ALTHOUGH THEY MAY BE COLORED DIFFERENTLY, SOME OF THESE ARE CHARACTERS I HAVE MET ON MY OTHER TRAVELS. THERE ARE ALSO SOME WHO APPEAR ELSEWHERE IN THIS BOOK. CAN YOU SPOT FOUR CHARACTERS THAT APPEAR TWICE IN THIS SPECTACULAR DISPLAY?

WHAT A DOG FIGHT!

BOW WOW WOW! TWO ARMIES ARE LOCKED IN BATTLE, ALL WITH DOG MASKS ON. ONE ARMY IS DRESSED IN BLUE, BLACK, AND WHITE, AND THE OTHER IN RED, BROWN, AND CREAM. CAN YOU FIND EIGHT SOLDIERS, FOUR FROM EACH SIDE, WITH SOMETHING IN ONE OF THE OTHER SIDE'S COLORS? OH, AND WHERE IS WOOF IN THIS DOG PACK?

THE BEAT OF THE DRUMS

BOOM BOOM BADOOM! WHAT AN ORDERLY SCENE! TWO ARMIES ARE STANDING AT ATTENTION, SMARTLY DRESSED IN PINK AND BLUE, BUT SOME SOLDIERS ARE LETTING THEIR SIDE DOWN! CAN YOU FIND THE SOLDIER WHO HAS FORGOTTEN HIS SOCKS AND BOOTS AND 16 SOLDIERS STICKING OUT THEIR TONGUES?

THE ENORMOUS PARTY

WOW! HOW EXCITING! ARE YOU IN THE MOOD FOR A PARTY, WALDO-WATCHERS? LOOK AT THE BALLOONS, THE STREAMERS, AND ALL THE SMILING FACES! THE FLAGS OF 18 COUNTRIES ARE FLYING HERE – CAN YOU SPOT SIX FLAGS THAT HAVE SOMETHING WRONG WITH THEM? *

* THE ANSWERS ARE AT THE BACK OF THIS BOOK. NO CHEATING!

WHERE'S WALDO? THE INCREDIBLE PAPER CHASE CHECKLIST

THE CASTLE SIEGE

- [ ] Five blue-coated soldiers wearing blue plumes
- [ ] Five red-coated soldiers wearing red plumes
- [ ] A blue-coated soldier wearing a red plume
- [ ] A red-coated soldier wearing a blue plume
- [ ] Four blue-coated archers
- [ ] Five characters holding white feathers
- [ ] Some pike men holding pikes
- [ ] Minors digging a tunnel
- [ ] Twenty-two ladders
- [ ] Some longbowmen wearing long bows
- [ ] Five catapults
- [ ] Twenty-seven ladies dressed in blue
- [ ] Twelve men with white beards
- [ ] A wishing well
- [ ] Two tidy witches
- [ ] Nine blue shields
- [ ] Four horses
- [ ] Three round red shields
- [ ] A prisoner in a puzzling position
- [ ] Eight men snoozing
- [ ] Someone with by far the longest hair
- [ ] A soldier with one bare foot
- [ ] Eighteen characters with their tongues out
- [ ] Five tents

THE JURASSIC GAMES

- [ ] A dinosaur volleyball game
- [ ] A dinosaur rowing race
- [ ] Dinosaurs playing cricket
- [ ] A dinosaur soccer match
- [ ] A dinosaur windsurfer race
- [ ] Dinosaurs playing baseball
- [ ] A dinosaur football game
- [ ] Dinosaurs playing basketball
- [ ] Dinosaurs playing golf
- [ ] A dinosaur steeplechase race
- [ ] A dinosaur polo match
- [ ] Four sets of dinosaur cheerleaders
- [ ] Dinosaurs keeping score with their tails
- [ ] Some show-jumping dinosaurs

PICTURE THIS

- [ ] A bird escaped from its frame
- [ ] An angry dragon
- [ ] An airplane with real wings
- [ ] An alarm clock
- [ ] A running cactus
- [ ] A rude tree trunk
- [ ] Some fish fingers
- [ ] A mermaid in reverse
- [ ] Three skiers
- [ ] A messy eater
- [ ] An upside-down picture
- [ ] A giant foot
- [ ] Three romantic animals
- [ ] A foot being tickled
- [ ] A picture within a picture
- [ ] Two men sharing the same hat
- [ ] Two helmets worn back-to-front
- [ ] Someone drinking through a straw
- [ ] Three flags
- [ ] Nine tongues hanging out
- [ ] A caveman escaped from his frame
- [ ] Seven dogs and a dogfish
- [ ] A bandaged finger
- [ ] A braided mustache
- [ ] Four bears
- [ ] Three helmets with red plumes
- [ ] Four cats
- [ ] Four ducks
- [ ] Yellow, blue, and red picture frames

THE GREAT RETREAT

- [ ] A shield suddenly vacated
- [ ] A heart on a soldier's tunic
- [ ] One curved sword
- [ ] A soldier carrying a hammer
- [ ] One striped spear
- [ ] A soldier not wearing a top
- [ ] Two runaway boots
- [ ] A horseless rider
- [ ] A soldier with a sword and an ax
- [ ] Three bare feet
- [ ] Four pink tails
- [ ] A spear with tips at both ends
- [ ] A helmet with a blue plume
- [ ] A soldier with a red boot and a blue boot
- [ ] A helmet with a red plume

MUDDY SWAMPY JUNGLE GAME

- [ ] An explorer with long sleeves
- [ ] An explorer carrying two spears
- [ ] An explorer wearing a shoe
- [ ] Four contented frogs
- [ ] An explorer with a white beard
- [ ] Five explorers not wearing tops
- [ ] A toe being nipped
- [ ] An explorer wearing a curled-up snake
- [ ] A belt buckled at the back
- [ ] An explorer with two cross-belts
- [ ] Ten butterflies
- [ ] A spear with tips at both ends
- [ ] Eight explorers pointing and laughing
- [ ] Three snapped spears

WHAT A DOG FIGHT!

- [ ] A gundog soldier
- [ ] A guard-dog soldier
- [ ] A boxer-dog soldier
- [ ] A bloodhound soldier
- [ ] A Great Dane soldier
- [ ] A prize poodle soldier
- [ ] Two soldiers begging for bones
- [ ] Two soldiers running to fetch a ball
- [ ] Four stars on one tunic
- [ ] A dog basket
- [ ] A dog wearing a man mask
- [ ] Two fellow soldiers fighting each other
- [ ] Four ticklish feet
- [ ] A howling dog soldier
- [ ] A soldier with two tails
- [ ] A white star on a cream tunic
- [ ] Cream eyes on a white dog mask
- [ ] A soldier with a black leg and a brown leg
- [ ] A soldier with a black arm and a cream arm
- [ ] A cream glove on a blue striped arm
- [ ] A cream glove on a black striped arm
- [ ] A brown dog mask on a blue tunic
- [ ] A blue nose on a brown dog mask

THE BEAT OF THE DRUMS

- [ ] A rude back row
- [ ] Courtesy causing a pile-up
- [ ] Some very short spears
- [ ] A group facing in all directions
- [ ] A collision about to happen
- [ ] A domino effect
- [ ] Spears held upside down
- [ ] A never-ending spear
- [ ] Two hats joined together
- [ ] Some very scruffy soldiers
- [ ] A soldier wearing only one shoe
- [ ] A soldier wearing red shoes
- [ ] Thirty-five horses
- [ ] A pink hatband and a blue hatband
- [ ] One blue spear
- [ ] One lost shoe
- [ ] One hat with a yellow feather
- [ ] One hat with a red hatband

THE GREAT ESCAPE

- Ten men wearing green hoods
- Ten men wearing only one glove
- Ten men wearing hoods not matching gloves
- Ten men wearing two different coloured gloves
- Ten men wearing short and long gloves
- Ten lost gloves
- Ten men wearing one fingerless glove
- Six ladders
- Nineteen shovels
- Five question mark shapes formed by the hedge

THE ENORMOUS PARTY

- Five back views of Waldo's head
- A servant bending over backward
- Two muscle-men being ignored
- An eight-man band
- A punctured tire
- A helmet worn backward
- Eight front wheels
- Two upside-down faces of Waldo
- A biker without a motorbike
- Seven red boots
- A man wrapped in a streamer
- A uniform that is too small
- A uniform that is too big
- Two men on one motorbike
- Someone wearing a red tie
- Someone wearing a blue beret
- A reluctant arm-rest

THE WACKY WALDO CIRCUS

- Four reluctant human cannonballs
- A clown wearing five hats
- A clown with a big honker
- A bandsman playing bagpipes
- A bespectacled family of four
- A bow tie in a clown's hair
- An icy ice-pop seller
- One man supporting three
- Three straws in one cup
- Two thirsty clowns
- A clown being used as a broom
- Three ketchup victims
- A boy with three drinks
- A man with six drinks
- Twelve clowns with flowers in their hats

THE ENORMOUS PARTY – ANSWERS

1 France
2 The Netherlands
3 United Kingdom
4 Sweden
5 Australia
6 Norway
7 Spain
8 Japan
9 Denmark

10 Switzerland
11 U.S.A.
12 Canada
13 Belgium
14 New Zealand
15 Finland
16 Austria
17 Germany
18 Brazil

FLAGS WITH FAULTS

3 Diagonal red stripes missing
4 Flying backward
5 One star missing
11 Red and white stripes reversed
12 Maple leaf upside-down
14 Diagonal red stripes missing

PENCIL AND PAPER

Did you find the ten tiny pieces of paper that Waldo dropped from his notepad—one in every scene? Waldo has also left his pencil somewhere on the journey—can you go back and find it, super-seekers?

AND TWO MORE THINGS!

Dozens of Waldo-watchers appear in this book (there is at least one in every scene, but some scenes have many more!).

There's another character—apart from Waldo, Woof, Wenda, Wizard Whitebeard, and Odlaw—in every scene. Can you find her?

STEP RIGHT UP! STEP RIGHT UP!
Be happy! Jump for joy!
Dance a dizzy dance!

The Wacky Waldo Circus
is in town!

THE WACKY WALDO CIRCUS
THE FOLLOWING PAGES ARE PURELY
FOR YOUR DELIGHT! FOLD OUT THE
PAGES AND PRESS OUT THE ACROBATS,
THE CLOWNS, AND THE PUPPETEERS....
TO PUT THE CIRCUS TOGETHER, LOOK
INSIDE THE ENVELOPE FOR HELP. NOW
INVITE YOUR FRIENDS, FAMILY, AND
PETS TO TAKE THEIR SEATS – THE
MORE, THE MERRIER! THEN STRIKE
UP THE BAND, HAND OUT THE
POPCORN, AND PUT ON YOUR
VERY OWN SHOW! WOW!